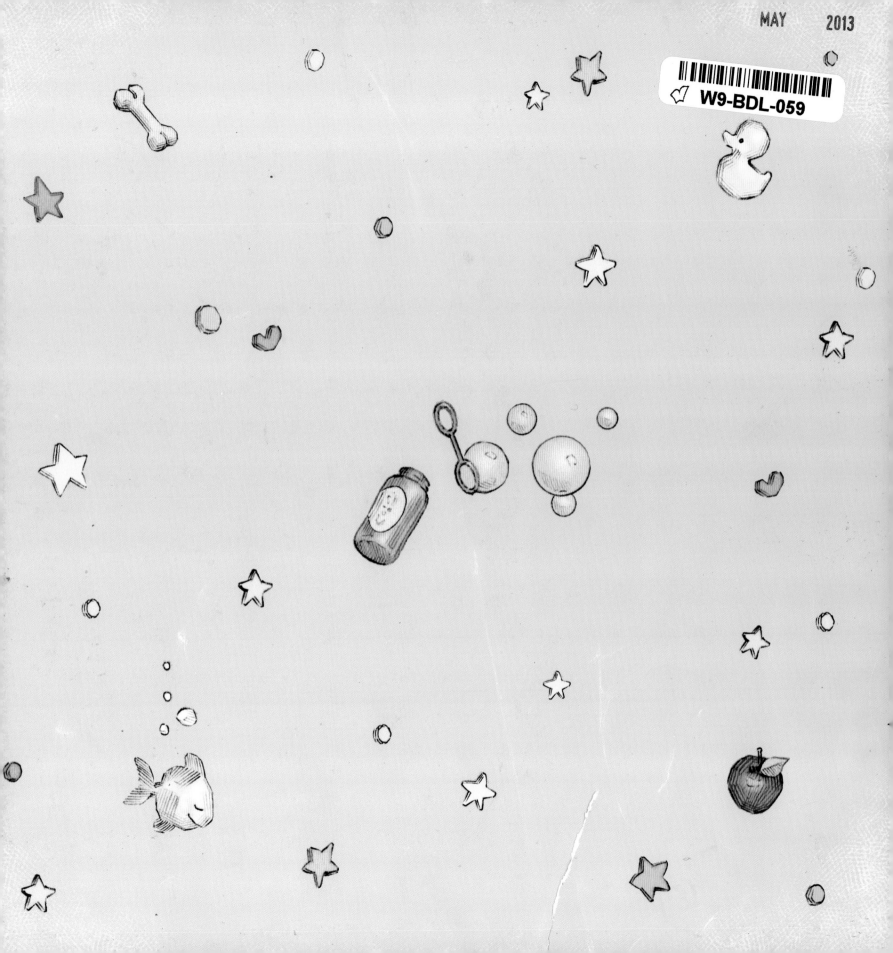

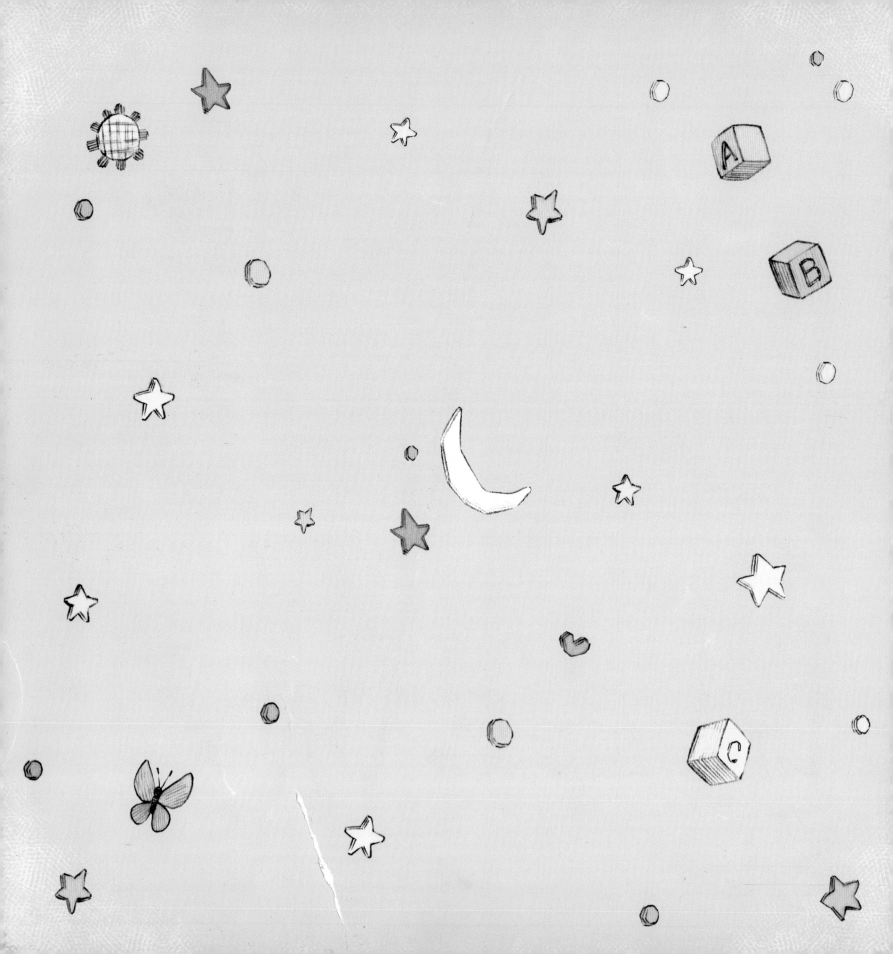

Someone's Sleepy

By Deborah Lee Rose

Illustrated by Dan Andreasen

Abrams Books for Young Readers, New York

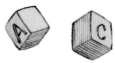

The art in this book was created using graphite, ink, and Adobe Photoshop.

Library of Congress Cataloging-in-Publication Data

Rose, Deborah Lee.
Someone's sleepy / by Deborah Lee Rose ; illustrated by Dan Andreasen.
p. cm.
ISBN 978-1-4197-0539-7 (alk. paper)
[1. Stories in rhyme. 2. Bedtime—Fiction. 3. Mother and child—Fiction.]
I. Andreasen, Dan, ill. II. Title. III. Title: Someone is sleepy.
PZ8.3.R714So 2013
[E]—dc23
2012015619

Printed and bound in China
10 9 8 7 6 5 4 3 2 1

ABRAMS
THE ART OF BOOKS SINCE 1949
115 West 18th Street
New York, NY 10011
www.abramsbooks.com

For Riley, Karsyn, Haley, Kamryn, Charlotte, Sylvie,
and Annabelle, and their very sleepy parents.
Special thanks to Tom Chapin for setting Someone's
Sleepy to music, and recording it as a lullaby —D.L.R.

For Katrina —D.A.

Stardust sky and silver moon
Someone's sleepy
Bedtime soon

Sleepy hands and sleepy feet
Sleepy neck that smells so sweet

Sleepy shoulders

Sleepy knees

Sleepy through-the-window breeze

Sleepy toes and fingertips

Sleepy quilt tucked all around
Sleepy world of nighttime sound

Sleepy mouth too tired to speak

Sleepy kisses on your cheek

Sleepy bear and bunny too
Sleepy hugs for all of you

Sleepy forehead

Sleepy nose

Sleepy eyes begin to close

Sleepy breath so soft and slow

Sleepy night-light's golden glow

Sleepy child in sleepy bed

Dream sweet dreams

My sleepyhead

Sleepy pillow smooth and deep
Someone's sleepy
Fast asleep.

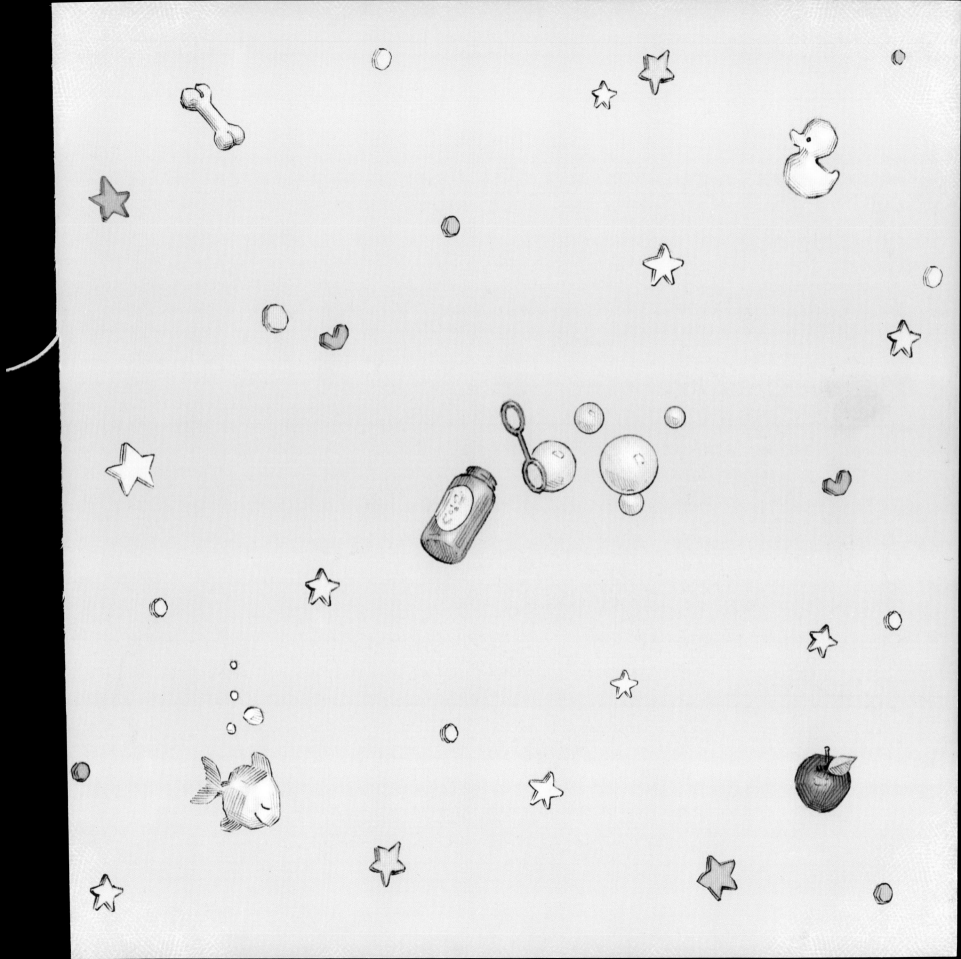

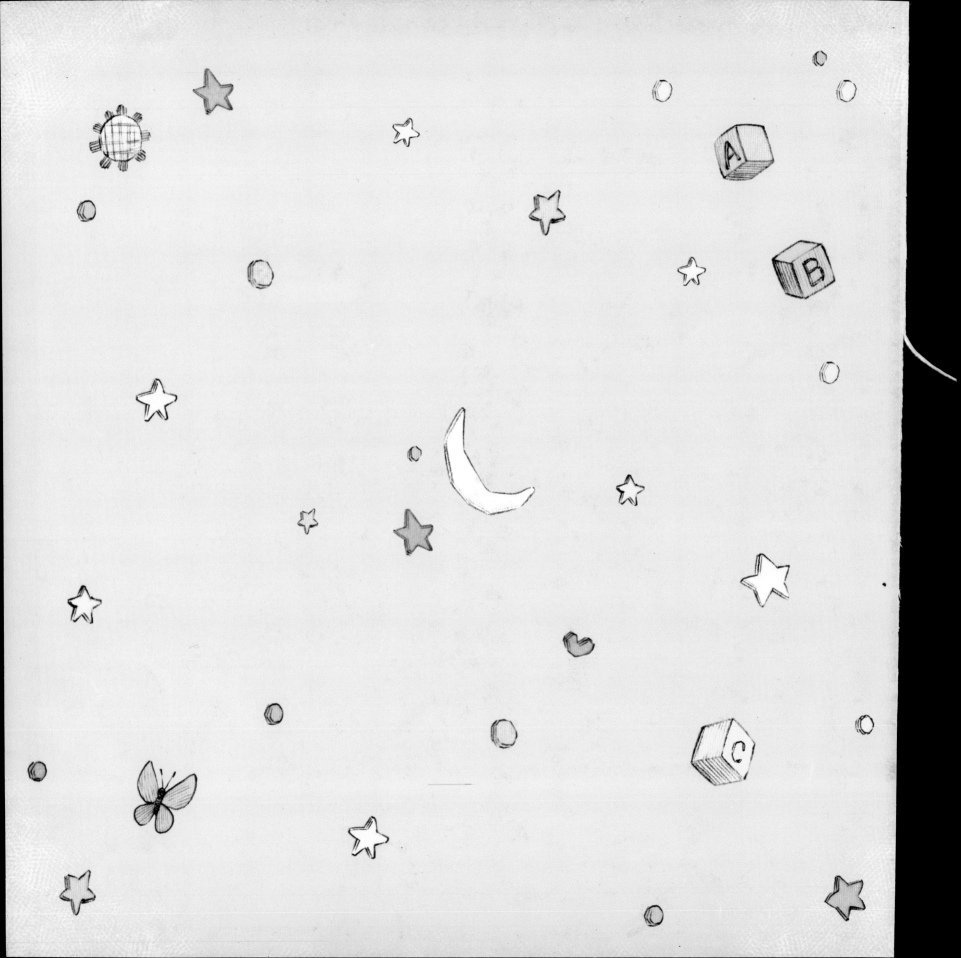